WARRIOR HEROES

HEROES

THE GLADIATOR'S
VICTORY

First published 2015 by A & C Black
An imprint of Bloomsbury Publishing Plc
50 Bedford Square, London WC1B 3DP

www.bloomsbury.com

Bloomsbury is a registered trademark of Bloomsbury Publishing Plc

ISBN 978-1-4729-0465-2

A CIP catalogue for this book is available from the British Library.

Printed and bound by CPI Group (UK) Ltd, Croydon CR0 4YY

1 3 5 7 9 10 8 6 4 2

WARRIOR HEROES

THE GLADIATOR'S VICTORY

BENJAMIN HULME-CROSS

Illustrated by
Angelo Rinaldi

A & C BLACK
AN IMPRINT OF BLOOMSBURY
LONDON NEW DELHI NEW YORK SYDNEY

CONTENTS

INTRODUCTION ~ The Hall of Heroes   7

CHAPTER 1   11

CHAPTER 2   21

~ Living in Rome   40

CHAPTER 3   43

~ Life as a Gladiator   57

CHAPTER 4   59

CHAPTER 5   70

~ Gladiator Types   86

CHAPTER 6   89

~ A Day at the Games   105

CHAPTER 7   107

CHAPTER 8   122

~ Origins of the Gladiators   131

CHAPTER 9   134

CHAPTER 10   150

INTRODUCTION
THE HALL OF HEROES

The Hall of Heroes is a museum
all about warriors throughout
history. It's full of swords, bows
and arrows, helmets, boats, armour,
shields, spears, axes and just
about anything else that a warrior
might need. But this isn't just
another museum full of old stuff
in glass cases - it's also haunted
by the ghosts of the warriors whose
belongings are there. Our great
grandfather, Professor Blade, set
up the museum and when he died he
started haunting the place too. He
felt guilty about the trapped ghost
warriors and vowed he would not
rest in peace until all the other
ghosts were laid to rest first. And
that's where Arthur and I come in...

On the night of the Professor's funeral Arthur and I broke into the museum – we knew it was wrong but we just couldn't help ourselves. And that's when we discovered something very weird. When we are touched by one of the ghost warriors we get transported to the time and place where the ghost lived and died. And we can't get back until we've fixed whatever it is that keeps the ghost from resting in peace. So we go from one mission to the next, recovering lost swords, avenging deaths, saving loved ones or doing whatever else the ghost warrior needs us to do.

Fortunately while the Professor was alive I wrote down everything he ever told us about these warriors in a book I call *Warrior Heroes* –

so luckily we do have some idea of what we're getting into each time - even if Arthur does still call me 'Finn the geek'. But we need more than a book to survive each adventure because wherever we go we're surrounded by war and battle and the fiercest fighters who ever lived, as you're about to find out!

CHAPTER 1

"Well chaps," said the Professor cheerfully. "What do you know about gladiators?"

Arthur's eyes nearly popped with delight, and even Finn, normally so anxious at the start of a new mission, could not disguise his excitement.

"We who are about to die, salute you!" Arthur chanted, thumping his chest with one hand

and holding the other out in front of him, thumb raised.

"The most highly skilled hand-to-hand warriors of all time," said Finn. "Trained in all sorts of combat styles just to entertain the public in Rome."

"Very good," said the Professor, laughing. "So you do pay attention to some of what I tell you. Mind you, thumbs up, you live, thumbs down, you die is probably a myth, and the 'we salute you' thing only happened once. But yes, they were specially trained to put on a show and fight in public."

"But I suppose they weren't *real* warriors," Finn mused as he looked around the Professor's study at the familiar military items that decorated the walls. "They were part of a public show all about fighting. Just like this museum is really. It was just a show wasn't it? Not the real thing."

"Well it was a sport, yes, but the fighting was real - often to the death in the early days."

"Of course they were *real* warriors!" Arthur cut in. "What about Spartacus? Wasn't he a gladiator?"

Finn looked at his brother, amazed that he knew who Spartacus was.

"What?" said Arthur noticing his brother's shocked expression. "I do know *some* things you know."

The Professor ignored the boys' squabbling and carried on, "Spartacus certainly was a real warrior. He led a whole army of escaped gladiators in an attack on Rome itself and very nearly won! Of course what he was escaping from was slavery. All the gladiators were slaves really – they were owned and traded, they were just treated better than other slaves because they were so valuable."

"But weren't they heroes as well?" Finn asked. "I thought that they were celebrities, like... footballers today."

"Quite a lot like footballers actually. They had short careers, earned huge sums of money, had crowds chanting their names from the stands of the amphitheatre, while they slugged it out in the arena at the centre. They were still slaves though, and Spartacus realised that an army of highly trained soldier-slaves who wanted to be free would be a formidable force. They were defeated eventually," the Professor sighed. "And most of them were crucified to set an example to other slaves, but they went down as heroes at the same time. The fact we all know the name Spartacus two thousand years later is proof enough!"

"And is that how our next warrior died?" Finn wondered out loud, a worried expression spreading across his face as he realised he and Arthur would soon be thrown into their next mission.

"Not at all. I don't know why he is not at rest. We think he was quite a celebrated gladiator actually. He died peacefully as far as we can tell, probably years after earning his freedom. But we'll find out soon – any minute now by the look of it."

Sure enough the atmosphere in the study had changed, just as it always did when one of the ghosts was about to enter. The lights flickered and the clock stopped ticking, the temperature dropped and all sound and motion ceased.

Arthur and Finn glanced at each other nervously, unsure what was about to enter the Professor's study, and dreading the worst. A dark shadow appeared as the door creaked slowly open. The warrior who strode in looked every bit the perfect fighter – a tall, muscular, fierce-looking man with a spear in his hand, a sword in his belt, and a plumed, shining helmet tucked under his arm. Yet despite his straight back and broad shoulders, something in his eyes seemed defeated.

He looked slowly around the room until his troubled gaze lighted on Arthur and Finn.

"I was a gladiator," he began. "A gladiator who

fought mostly at the Flavian Amphitheatre
in Rome. My name was Marcus and I was
an equite."

"Gladiator on a horse," Finn whispered
to Arthur.

"My brother..." Marcus went on, and Finn guessed silently that this would be another mission to avenge someone's death. "My brother died with Spartacus, you know."

"Your brother and thousands more besides!" said the Professor. "You have our sincere sympathies, although I doubt that we will be able to reverse the outcome of that particular war..."

"No, it is true," said the gladiator. "They were destined to lose but I would not change any of that. My brother died fighting for a principle - for freedom. I had the chance to fight for the same thing and I ignored it. I chose to stay when he escaped and I fought on in the arena. I earned my freedom eventually, but along the way I killed many people as a gladiator. I was not fighting for a principle, I was fighting to save my own skin, and to entertain the crowds." Marcus paused here and gripped the side of the open door, with his head bent low.

"As soon as I heard of my brother's death I wished that I had escaped with him and fought alongside Spartacus. If there had been more of us things might have been different..."

"And what is it that you would change about your life if you could?" asked Finn.

"I would take the chance to fight for something real, the chance to show nobility, that is all..."

Finn and Arthur exchanged another nervous glance. This was a less specific request than usual and might be hard to get right. However, Marcus had no more to say and in two long strides had crossed the room and placed a hand on each boy's shoulder. The air in the room shifted, and seemed to fill with mist, drifting at first and then whirling faster and faster around them until the study could not be seen and it felt to the boys as if they were spinning through the sky...

CHAPTER 2

"You're going to get a beating boy! I said stand up!" Arthur heard the words as if he were listening through a thick wall. As he slowly opened his eyes and began to take in his surroundings, he became sharply aware of a terrible stench filling his nostrils. Looking up, he saw that he was lying in a narrow alleyway, hemmed in by tall buildings on either side.

The stench, he soon realised, came from the mounds of rotting food and sewage that muddied the ground.

"Where am I?" Arthur groaned to nobody, pushing himself up on his elbow and blinking up at a dusty, orange sky.

"You're on my patch, boy," a harsh voice replied, and Arthur twisted round slowly to see a rough, scarred, street-wise looking teenager glaring down at him, slapping the end of what seemed to be a well-used club into the palm of his hand. "I'm Festus. And that's all you need to know. Now get up and tell me why you're here or by Jupiter I'll crush your skull before you say another word."

Suddenly, Arthur didn't feel so blurry-eyed. He dragged himself quickly to his feet and held his hands up, noticing for the first time that a gang of similarly menacing boys stood behind Festus.

"I... I'm new here. I don't know where I am," Arthur spluttered, still slightly confused and trying to buy time. He held out little hope of out-fighting or out-running the gang.

"You're on my patch, boy," Festus repeated with a sneer. "This is Rome. Welcome to the greatest city in the world," he added sarcastically.

"Er... Thanks," said Arthur, stepping forward warily. "Now if you'll just let me past I'll be on my way and get off your patch."

Festus stood motionless. "What do you think lads?"

"Let's teach him a lesson," one of the gang called back, and the rest began cheering.

Arthur's heart sank. He tried to think of a way out of this situation. Only one idea came to mind and it was risky, but he had to find a way out of this mess. Taking a deep breath and puffing out his chest, he glared at the gang.

"Cowards!" he shouted, and the cheering stopped instantly. Festus' face darkened, and he stepped a little closer to Arthur.

"You think we're cowards? We'll see who's begging for mercy in a minute shall we?"

"Well if you're not a coward then let's make this a fair fight," said Arthur, praying that this challenge would work. "Me against the best you've got. One on one. No weapons. Unless you only fight in packs when your victim can't fight back of course..."

"You don't know what you're doing boy,"

Festus growled. "But you asked for it and you're going to get it. I'll fight you and by the time I've finished you'll wish I'd set the whole gang on you."

"We'll see," said Arthur, raising his fists. "But if I win, that's it. You let me go."

"Agreed." Festus nodded. "You won't win though. And we won't fight here in an alley – we need some space." He turned his back on Arthur and pushed his way back through the gang. "Bring him to the arena," he barked. Arthur had just a moment to realise that his plan had worked before he found himself being frogmarched along the alley, surrounded by Festus' gang.

* * *

Some distance away Finn sat up in an empty alley and rubbed his eyes, wincing as a foul smell and a loud, metallic banging sound assaulted his senses. Like Arthur, it always took him a few minutes to remember where he was and why he was there when he first woke up in a new time. Looking around for clues Finn noted that the stinking alley ran between two dismal-looking apartment blocks, at one end of which there seemed to be a lighter, busier, more open space.

He stretched, pushed himself to his feet and cautiously made his way along the alley, emerging into a very shabby market square. The sides of the square were lined with tables, benches and grubby wooden shacks most of which seemed to serve as shops. Others, judging by the raucous voices of the men at the tables, were bars.

Cautiously, Finn began walking around the perimeter of the square, staying in the shadows and trying not to draw attention to himself. He took a closer look at the men's tunics and instantly remembered what he was there for. Rome! The gladiator! Freedom! The satisfaction of remembering the mission was quickly overtaken by a feeling of surprise. This wasn't how Finn expected Rome to look. It looked too – modern. Behind the shops that lined the square, the apartment blocks rose five or six stories up to tiled rooftops.

"Prepare the arena for Festus!" someone shouted, interrupting his thoughts. *An arena?* Finn glanced around in confusion, looking for anything that might resemble a gladiator's arena. Some of the men at the tables began cheering and laughing. From an alley on the opposite side of the square Finn saw a gang of teenagers spilling out past a bar and into the middle of the square. *Where's the arena?* Finn wondered, and then he groaned as he saw a smaller boy being marched along, held tight by two of the gang members. Arthur.

"How does he do this every time?" Finn hissed to himself, furious that his brother had yet again damaged their chances of success by getting into trouble and making a spectacle of himself within minutes of arriving. He watched, dismayed, as Arthur was pushed along into the middle of the square, the gang calling over to the men to join them as they formed a human circle around him. Several of the men put their cups down and obliged. Finn guessed that the 'arena' for this gang just meant any piece of ground where they could fight.

"And who do we have here?" one of them shouted.

"This little runt challenged Festus to a fight!" one of the gang replied. *Challenged*? Finn's stomach tightened with worry and anger.

"Still fighting lambs eh Festus? You'll make a great gladiator one day!" the man jeered, and his friends chuckled. It seemed that Festus was not held in very high regard by the men, Finn mused.

A tough-looking, scarred teenager stepped forward from the circle and turned to face the men. "Lamb or wolf," he growled, swinging a club menacingly. "No one challenges me on my patch and gets away with it!"

"No weapons," Finn heard Arthur call out. "We agreed. Or do you only fight when you have an unfair advantage?" Finn began to see what had happened. Maybe Arthur hadn't been so stupid after all. Nonetheless, Finn didn't fancy his brother's chances against this thug. Scanning the sides of the market square, Finn began to think about how he might help Arthur escape. He noticed a grizzled giant of a man standing alone in the shadows, observing the gang silently. Something about him seemed too dangerous to Finn and he decided against asking him for help. Maybe the drinkers were a better bet. He sidled up to stand next to the man who had taunted Festus and hoped he would agree to help him.

* * *

"Come on Festus," one of the gang cheered. "Teach him a lesson."

Arthur looked over at the men who were watching, grinned and then bleated like a lamb, sending the men into fits of laughter. The more people he could get on his side the better. Festus hurled his club to the floor and charged at Arthur without warning. Calmly, as if he had known it would happen, Arthur stepped to one side, leaving a foot trailing so that Festus tripped and tumbled to the ground. The men cheered and Festus sprang, snarling, to his feet. Arthur could see that his opponent was much stronger than him. His only hope was to keep Festus so enraged that he couldn't think clearly. As the thug advanced more carefully towards him, Arthur began dancing sideways around the circle as if he were in a boxing ring, bleating even more comically. Glaring malevolently, Festus crouched low and circled with him, waiting for his chance.

Arthur could see real hatred in the boy's eyes now as Festus prowled, feinting with mini-lunges now and then but never breaking eye-contact. The cheers and laughter of the spectators faded as Arthur focussed all his attention on the fight. When the next attack came it was far more controlled. Festus stepped forward, feigned as if to punch Arthur in the stomach and then dropped to one knee, grabbing hold of Arthur's ankle and giving it a vicious twist. Arthur tumbled to the ground and Festus pounced, pinning him down with an arm across his chest and punching him hard on the chin.

Ignoring the pain in his bruised chin, Arthur twisted his head one way and the other trying to dodge the blows until Festus pulled his arm right back to deliver the killer punch.

Sensing that the weight across his chest had lightened slightly Arthur slid a few inches to one side and snapped his head out of the way just as Festus brought his fist down with all his weight behind it. The blow glanced off the side of Arthur's head and thumped into the mud, drawing a cry of pain from Festus, whose momentum sent him sprawling. Seizing his opportunity, Arthur rolled out from under his opponent and leapt to his feet, aiming a swift kick at Festus' ribs just as the older boy pushed himself up.

Festus howled with anger and crashed forward once more, throwing another massive punch. Arthur weaved to one side, grabbed Festus' wrist in both hands and twisted as the punch carried the older boy forwards and past Arthur.

Now Arthur was in complete control, standing behind Festus and twisting his arm up behind his back. He curled a foot in front of Festus and pushed, sending him crashing to the floor. This time Arthur went with him, still holding Festus' twisted arm and landing on his back so that the older boy could not move.

The men clapped and cheered as Festus' gang looked darkly on.

"It's over Festus!" said the man standing next to Finn, laughing. "You took on the mighty lamb, and the lamb won!"

Arthur looked down at his opponent. "Are we done?"

Festus nodded, grunting in the mud and Arthur rolled away.

* * *

Swallowing his nerves, Finn tapped the man next to him on the arm. "Excuse me sir," he said.

"What is it boy?" the man barked, glancing at Finn for the first time. "You want a go too?"

"No!" Finn replied hurriedly. "I'm no match. But this lamb-boy put up a good fight didn't he?"

"Not bad," the man nodded. "Not bad at all."

"Then we'll make sure the gang let him go, sir?"

Before the man could reply there was a cheer from the gang as Festus lunged for the club he had thrown to the floor and charged at Arthur once more, swinging wildly.

"*Hey!*" Finn shouted. "*Leave him alone!*"

A few of the gang members turned on Finn and shoved him backwards, knocking him into the older man.

"The boy's right," shouted the man. "The lamb won fair and square. Let him go."

"No chance!" Festus yelled.

"Are you going to let them talk to you like that?" asked Finn.

"No," snarled the man as he started pushing forwards to get through the gang to Festus. He was joined by several of the other men. The gang's circle disintegrated and a brawl broke out as fists and boots and knees and heads connected with each other. Finn dodged his way through the blows as well as he could, desperate to reach Arthur, who he could see was struggling to avoid Festus' club now that so many other bodies were filling the space.

"*I said leave him alone!*" Finn shouted, darting

forward and leaping onto Festus' back. Festus staggered backwards and then fell forward to the floor yet again. Arthur rushed forwards and stamped on Festus' arm. He dropped the club and roared in pain.

"To me, boys!" Festus called, thrashing his elbows around to shake Finn off and jumping to his feet. But as he did so Finn just grinned at him.

"It's over Mr Wolf," Finn mocked. "Your friends have had enough." They were surrounded now by a ring of the older men as the last of the gang members scurried and limped away into the alleys. Festus' shoulders slumped.

"Get out of here!" ordered the man Finn had been talking to. Festus needed no second bidding and darted away towards one of the alleys.

Arthur and Finn looked around at the circle of men.

"Thanks!" they both said at once. It was only then that Finn noticed that the giant who had been watching from the shadows earlier had joined the circle of men. The huge brute stepped forward and the others, also noticing him for the first time, began to sidle away.

"You two!" he boomed. "The games begin next week and I'm looking for fighters. We need to talk."

EXTRACT FROM *WARRIOR HEROES*

BY FINN BLADE

LIVING IN ROME

HOUSING

The population of ancient Rome
was around 800,000, making it by
far the largest city in the world at
that time. These people would have
led very different lives from those
living elsewhere.

Most people lived in apartments
and many of the streets were lined
with apartment blocks that were up
to eight stories high. They were
made of wood and bricks, or an early
form of concrete, and had tiled
roofs. But many of them were built
cheaply by money-grabbing landlords,
and people often died when the
buildings collapsed.

SHOPS

In busy streets and market squares, the rooms at the bottom of each block of apartments were shops and bars, just like you see in cities today.

WATER

The Romans built raised canals called aqueducts to pipe fresh water down into the city from clean rivers in the hills. The clean water fed the public drinking fountains and the public baths.

BATHS

Unless you were very rich, or very poor, you would have used the public baths in Rome. These had steam rooms, swimming pools, and areas for wrestling and games - like leisure centres today, but made of marble. Oh, and everyone walked around naked at the baths!

TOILETS

Most people also used public toilets. There were no cubicles, so they really were public! Sewage sloshed away through underground sewers and out into the river Tiber.

CHAPTER 3

Arthur yawned and rubbed his shoulder. It was three days since Gaius had told them he wanted a new training partner for one of the young gladiators at the school. Gaius, who as lanista ruled the gladiators and oversaw their training, had been impressed by what he saw when Arthur fought Festus. He had also spotted Finn talking to the men to make sure that Arthur got out alive after winning his fight, and he had asked both boys to come with him to the gladiator school.

Finn had stared around in awe as Gaius led them from Festus' 'arena', through the streets of Rome to the gladiator school. No number of history lessons on Rome could have prepared him for the sheer scale of the city. They passed domed, marble temples, huge victory arches, and statues perched atop soaring stone columns. Clean, oiled men in togas emerged from public baths, shopkeepers shouted at slaves, small groups congregated in the heat beside beautiful public drinking fountains. Again Finn had found himself marvelling at how modern it all felt.

Quite what Gaius had in mind for Finn remained a mystery, but when they arrived at the compound of the gladiator school, Arthur had been set to work immediately, sparring with Gaius and with other trainers, and as soon as he entered the cell he slumped down onto his mattress. Gaius had been putting his new recruit through his paces and Arthur felt more bruised and broken than at any time in his life. Finn smiled across at him.

"Hard day?"

"It's alright for you!" said Arthur bitterly. "You haven't had to do anything!"

"Yeah," Finn snorted, "Look at all this luxury. I can do whatever I want!" The tiny cell they were in was more of a prison cell than anything else. The two thin mattresses on the floor were the only things in the room.

"At least the stone walls keep us cool I suppose,"

Finn went on, trying to find something positive to say about their situation. "Anyway, I can't help it if I'm the brains and you're the brawn. It's going well. We're inside the gladiator school and it's only a matter of time before we meet Marcus. Then all we have to do is persuade him to fight for his freedom so he dies happy!"

"And when we do finally meet Marcus," said Arthur with a yawn as he stretched out on the mattress. "What are we going to say to him?"

Finn paused and frowned, "I've been thinking about that. It looks like it will probably be you who meets Marcus, and when it happens, you may not have much time to talk to him."

"That's if he'll even talk to me at all." There was a short silence as the boys pondered the difficulties they would face in persuading a gladiator who saw them as total strangers to plan an escape and fight for his principles. "How will I even make him listen to anything I've got to say?"

"You need to try and establish a connection straight away," said Finn. "Persuade him you're not really a total stranger after all. Either that or just get him thinking about his brother - that's what this is all about. Marcus died regretting that he didn't fight for his freedom like his brother. It must have played on his mind his whole life. Try and leave Marcus with thoughts of his brother and Spartacus."

"Then what?" said Arthur, looking unconvinced.

"Then we'll have to give him something to fight for, obviously!"

A loud thump on the door of the boys' cell

prevented them talking further, and Gaius ducked through the doorway.

"How are the muscles?" he flashed Arthur a quick smile. Arthur puffed out his cheeks and Gaius laughed. "You'd better get used to it. Tomorrow you begin sparring with Ajax."

Gaius had already explained to Arthur that Ajax was his top young gladiator. Little more than a boy himself at fifteen, Ajax was scheduled to fight another teenager from the same gladiator school in the public arena the following week.

"I never asked, who was he sparring with before you found me?"

"There was an accident," came Gaius' unblinking reply. "We needed someone new, and Ajax needs to learn some control." Arthur's eyes widened and his mouth dropped open.

"Finn," Gaius went on before Arthur could reply. "Come with me. Your work starts tonight."

Casting a nervous glance back at Arthur, Finn got to his feet and followed the huge lanista out of the cell and across the open space of the training arena to a gate in the walls of the compound. Gaius paused at the gate.

"Put this on," he commanded, throwing a cloak at Finn. "And keep the hood up."

"But I'm not cold," Finn protested.

"It's not to keep you warm boy, it's to keep you hidden. Come, I'll tell you as much as I know on the way."

"On the way where?" Finn asked nervously, wrapping the cloak around his shoulders and pulling the hood up.

"Stop asking questions!" Gaius snapped. "I said

I'll explain on the way. Now follow me." Gaius looked at Finn's hood, grunted with approval and opened the gate of the gladiator school, stepping through it and out onto the dark street outside. He set off briskly, with Finn almost running to keep up and doing his best to memorise their route as they cut through fetid, muddy alleyways, across squares and eventually out onto a busier, paved road that was seething with activity. Carts and chariots rumbled along the road. Whips cracked. Crowds jostled. Beggars cried out, and Finn could think of nothing beyond staying close to Gaius.

After what seemed like an eternity they left the main road and the crowd thinned out. Gaius suddenly said, "We're going to see Lucius. Listen and remember. Lucius is a senator. He owns the gladiator school, which means he owns you. Lucius has many rivals in the senate but there is one man who is a particular threat to him. His name is Titus and he owns another gladiator school. Lucius believes that Titus plans to have him assassinated. He needs someone loyal to infiltrate Titus' household."

"To do what?" Finn enquired.

"I don't know boy, that's what we're going to find out. It was not just a sparring partner for Ajax that I was looking for when I found you and your brother. It was someone smart. Someone whose face would not be recognised. Someone who could be a spy."

Finn swallowed dryly. All this was taking him further and further away from Arthur and Marcus and into seriously dangerous territory.

In any case, with no knowledge of Rome, Finn couldn't see how he would be any use as a spy.

Finn's nerves finally got the better of him and without knowing what he was doing he blurted out, "Wait! There's something you need to know." Gaius stopped and stared at him steadily. "I'm not from Rome. Arthur and I only just got here. I don't know the streets or the people or the customs."

"You think I hadn't noticed that boy?" Gaius snorted. "But you're smart. Can you remember the way back to the gladiator school?" Finn thought for a moment and then began to describe the way back. Gaius nodded. "And you were smart enough to get a bunch of drunk soldiers on your side to look out for your brother the other day."

"Yes, but..."

"But nothing!" Gaius snapped. "Lucius needs someone with no connections. He needs someone whose face has never been seen before. He needs someone who will arouse no suspicions. You say you don't know Rome? Well know this, Rome is a city of thieves and liars, and the greater the rank the greater the lies. Deep down every senator fears he will one day be assassinated by a rival, and probably one who claimed to be a friend. If you were from Rome, Lucius couldn't trust you."

"But he's never even met me. How can he trust me in any case?"

"Well I suppose that's why he wants to meet you tonight," said Gaius. "And of course he knows that you care about your brother..."

There was no threat in Gaius' tone, but Finn

couldn't ignore the implied warning, and as Gaius set off along the road once more Finn shivered and followed silently. As they walked an intriguing question began to form in Finn's mind. *What happens to Lucius' gladiators if he is assassinated?* Finn had no idea, and he wasn't about to ask, but it seemed to him that the sudden death of Lucius might be the perfect catalyst for an escape attempt by some of his gladiators, or even just one...

"This is the back of the house." Gaius' voice cut in. They were standing by a simple door in a high wall, flanked by a pair of sullen-looking guards. "Don't ask questions. Don't look at Lucius unless he's talking to you. And don't even think about suggesting you're not up to the job. Is that understood?"

Finn nodded and Gaius muttered something to the guards, who rapped on the door, and, when it swung inwards, waved them through.

The contrast between the grubby street and the oasis they entered took Finn's breath away. They were standing in a covered stone walkway that ran around the perimeter of a beautiful, sweet-smelling garden; at one end of which stood the most stunning house Finn had ever seen. Through the arches of the walkway Finn could make out elegant statues, lush plants and a magnificent fountain. Finn had almost forgotten why he was there and it was a few moments before he noticed that a male slave in a simple tunic stood waiting for them.

"Is your master ready for us?" asked Gaius. The slave nodded, and led the way silently towards the house. They entered, stopping outside an intricately carved door and Finn gazed around at a cool, clean world of marble as the slave made a guttural coughing sound.

"Enter!" came a thin, high reply.

At that moment Finn was suddenly very aware of the many dangers he and Arthur faced in their quest to free Marcus. Not only did they have to find Marcus and persuade him to escape with two boys he had never met before, but Arthur also had to survive brutal combat as a gladiator's sparring partner and Finn was about to meet one of the most powerful men in Rome – the man who owned them all. Finn swallowed hard as Gaius pushed him towards the door.

EXTRACT FROM *WARRIOR HEROES*
BY FINN BLADE

LIFE AS A GLADIATOR

Gladiators were trained and housed
in schools by a lanista, who was a
bit like a brutal sergeant major.
The lanista had to know that the
gladiators would put on a good
show and fight bravely. They needed
finely tuned fighting skills, but
they also needed to be tough enough
to fight on bravely even if they
were losing, or injured. The lanista
also had to know that if they were
instructed to do so, they would kill
their enemy after defeating him. So
the training, as you can imagine,
was extremely tough!

CELEBRITY

Sometimes the gladiators from a

particular owner would be hired out for shows in other cities, so the best gladiators became famous all over the empire. They were portrayed in art and literature, and you can still see some of their names carved into walls around Rome. Add to that the fact that they performed in huge stadiums before fans screaming their names, and you can see why they were the sporting celebrities of their day.

SLAVES

However despite their fame, most were slaves and so had very low social status, although they might earn their freedom after years of glorious battle, and they could retire wealthy as they were often allowed to keep much of the prize money they won.

CHAPTER 4

The meeting was brief but supremely unsettling. Lucius, a bony, middle-aged man with a cruel mouth, stood in the centre of the room, the white cloth of his toga brushing the floor. He studied Finn in silence as Finn stared at the man's sandals.

"Let me see your face," Lucius instructed, and something in the man's tone made Finn's stomach turn as he pulled back his hood.

"He's very young," the senator commented, walking forward and putting a soft, moist hand under Finn's chin. "Look at me boy." Finn did so, trying hard to resist the urge to brush the repellent man's hand aside.

"Do you wish any harm to befall your brother?" he asked quietly, never taking his eyes from Finn's. Finn swallowed and shook his head.

"Of course not," Lucius went on. "Then do not fail me."

Finn nodded, speechless.

"Those who fail me are punished, do you understand boy?" He gestured towards the slave who had shown Finn in as he said this. The slave grimaced and opened his mouth. Finn's eyes widened. He couldn't be certain, but it seemed that the slave was missing his tongue. Finn blinked and looked back at Lucius, nodding quickly.

"Good. You may go. Gaius will instruct you presently. Wait for him in the garden."

Finn stumbled back out of the house, his hands over his mouth, and sat down heavily on a stone bench as his thoughts and fears whirled. He and Arthur had no plan for an escape attempt with Marcus – they had not even met him yet – and now Marcus' owner was effectively holding Arthur hostage. And what a sinister man. Finn shivered with loathing at the all too fresh memory of Lucius' terrible, soft voice in his ear and the thought of the slave's injury. When a hand touched his shoulder he jumped off the bench with a hoarse cry, flinging an elbow back as he did so.

He spun round, fists clenched, only to find himself eye-to-eye with a startled-looking girl.

"I'm sorry," they both said at once, and then laughed as a little of the tension evaporated.

"I am Lucilla," said the girl. "My apologies, I shouldn't have surprised you."

"Not your fault," Finn replied. "I'm just a bit distracted at the moment. I'm Finn."

The girl walked around to the front of the bench and sat down, motioning to Finn to do the same.

"Most people are nervous after meeting my uncle. He has that effect on people."

"Your uncle?" Finn gulped, instantly back on guard as Lucilla nodded forlornly.

"I wish he were not. He is not a good man – but I think you might know that already. You are the boy who will spy on Titus?" Finn froze, not sure how to respond. "I'm not supposed to know, but I make it my business to find out what my uncle is planning when it comes to Titus. I hear that you are not from Rome, so perhaps I can trust you." Lucilla paused and her face clouded over as she muttered, "I am to marry Titus."

"What? How old are you?" Finn blurted,

confused. "And isn't Titus your uncle's enemy?"

"I am twelve years old, and yes, Titus and my uncle are rivals. I am a peace offering, I think." Even in the middle of all his own troubles, Finn found himself feeling quite sorry for Lucilla.

Casting a furtive glance over her shoulder, Lucilla continued briskly, "Listen, we don't have long. I am just asking that if you discover anything that puts my marriage to Titus in doubt you will get word to me. Marrying Titus will get me away from my uncle and I have to escape this house one way or another."

"Why?" Finn asked.

Lucilla's face darkened further. "I just have to. I hate him. If I could kill him without getting caught I would but he is very, very careful. He kills anyone who gets in his way yet no-one can kill him. He poisons people – did you know that? He poisoned my parents..."

She was interrupted by the sound of footsteps and jumped up quickly from the bench.

"Goodbye for now Finn," Lucilla whispered, and slipped away just before Gaius and the slave emerged from the house.

* * *

An hour later Finn was standing face to face with Titus, a knot of fear in his stomach. Lucius' instructions could not have been clearer or more sinister: *Kill Titus and Arthur lives.* Gaius had met Finn in the garden after Lucilla had disappeared and delivered the instruction in a strained voice. He clearly was not happy about something – whether it was the plan to assassinate Titus or the fact that Lucius was using a boy to do the work, Finn could not tell. Gaius had placed a cord with a small bottle hanging from it around Finn's neck. Poison was Lucius' weapon of choice, just as Lucilla had said.

As Finn followed Gaius' directions to Titus' villa, he had become more and more certain that the fix for everyone's problems was for Lucius to be killed. Finn didn't like the idea of doing this himself, but he wasn't sure he had much choice.

Lucilla would be free of the terrible uncle who had murdered her parents. Arthur and Finn would be free of the man who was effectively holding them hostage. And Marcus might well be prompted to fight for his freedom too. It was a risky strategy, but it was also the only one that seemed to lead in the right direction. Following this logic, Finn had decided that the only thing he could do was approach Titus with complete honesty, and when he arrived at the villa he had announced that he was there to warn Titus about an attempt on his life. He had been escorted under guard to a room not unlike the one in which he had met Lucius.

However the man who stared back at him could not have been more different to Lucius. Tall, strong and with something noble in his demeanour, Titus displayed none of Lucius' reptilian menace. He listened to Finn's explanation of events without interruption, and he continued staring at Finn long after the boy had finished speaking.

"Show me the poison," he said at length. Swallowing nervously, Finn removed the bottle from around his neck and handed it over. Titus removed the stopper and waved the liquid under his nose, nodding slowly before closing the bottle and placing it on a table. "Let me be sure that I fully understand the facts," he went on. "Your brother is in training to be a gladiator. You were recruited to poison me and were told that your brother would pay dearly if you failed. And Lucilla wants to escape Lucius because she knows that he killed her parents."

Finn nodded, praying that he had not misjudged the situation.

"And you are telling me this because you hope that in return for your honesty I may help you."

Finn nodded again.

"Then you are either very brave, or very stupid, or both," said Titus quietly and paused. Finn's heart pounded. Titus studied Finn carefully and continued, "I can see no reason for you to invent any of this, so this is what we will do..."

CHAPTER 5

" Arthur," Gaius called, "It's time."

Stomach lurching, Arthur followed Gaius across the sand to the middle of the training arena. Arthur's fighting skills were impressive. He had fought with Vikings, Samurai, knights and many more, learning from each of them. But despite training with Gaius, Arthur still did not feel ready to fight a properly trained gladiator –

even if they were just supposed to be sparring. He wondered how Finn was faring. His brother had told him all about the meeting with Lucius and the assassination plot, and had set off earlier that morning.

"Remember," Gaius cut in gruffly, interrupting Arthur's worries. "Ajax is a secutor. His weapons and armour are stronger than yours but they are also heavier. If you show the same speed that you used against Festus the other day then you can give Ajax a good run. Now, let's check your gear." Gaius ran his hands over Arthur's light defences – a shoulder guard, a leg guard and an arm guard, nodding as he did so.

"One more thing Arthur. Ajax is a good fighter but he has a nasty temper. Just remember this is a sparring bout and don't end up starting a war. Ajax is fighting for real in the arena tomorrow for the first time. He needs practice today but I don't want him getting injured, do you understand?"

Arthur nodded, curling his fingers more tightly around his net and trident. As a retiarius these were his only weapons save for the dagger in his belt and as the lanista led him out into the arena he couldn't help feeling that he was the only one who was going to come out of this bout injured. If what Gaius had implied about Ajax's last sparring partner was correct then he'd be lucky to get out alive, let alone unscathed.

"Wait here," said Gaius. Arthur looked around the now very familiar training arena. Three of the four sides of the compound were lined with long rows of cells so that the arena was the first thing every gladiator saw when he woke up in the morning. The smooth, dusty compound walls were about twice the height of a man – high enough that you couldn't climb over them in any case. Several older gladiators stood watching in the early morning sun. One of them nodded at Arthur and smiled. Marcus! Arthur realised with a start. Maybe this was his chance to make contact. The thought had gone before he even registered it. Across the compound a door opened, and through it Arthur caught sight of the gladiator he was about to fight.

He gulped. If Ajax was fifteen then he was a monster. He was massive, even next to the huge, curved, rectangular shield he carried. A smooth bronze helmet covered his whole head and face, the gleaming metal broken by two small eye-holes through which Arthur could see only darkness staring back at him. He looked like some sort of demonic warrior from a nightmare and Arthur shuddered, suddenly very aware of the air on his unprotected face as Ajax swung his heavy sword through the air again and again in huge circles.

"Now boys," Gaius instructed. "You're only sparring but I want a proper fight all the same. Until I say stop you keep fighting and you fight to win. The instant I say stop you stop. Any repeat of last time Ajax and I'll have you whipped. Do I make myself clear? Now..." the lanista broke off and turned as he heard footfalls behind him. "Lucius sir. This is an unexpected honour."

Arthur tried hard not to stare at the man

Finn had spoken of with so much loathing the previous night.

"Carry on!" said Lucius as he flicked his hands at the boys. "Final preparations for the bouts taking place today and tomorrow eh Gaius? I thought I would come and inspect my gladiators before our moment of glory arrives. I see Marcus is looking well. Come here man."

Marcus walked obediently forward and Lucius placed a hand on the gladiator's arm. Arthur got the impression that Marcus was gritting his teeth.

"You will do me proud this afternoon eh Marcus? A fine specimen like you – it is on days such as these that a gladiator repays his master in glory." Lucius said with a simpering smile on his face.

"I am here to serve, master," Marcus replied stiffly, staring straight ahead.

"Quite so," said Lucius. "You are all here to serve me, and the citizens of Rome. And where is our latest recruit Gaius? The boy?" Arthur groaned inside as Gaius guided Lucius in his direction.

"My dear Gaius," Lucius snorted, squeezing Arthur's arm. "He really is just a boy isn't he?"

"He can fight, sir."

"Well," said Lucius, looking long and hard at Arthur. "I'll have to take your word. Let us hope that no significant harm befalls him eh? I see that Ajax is looking primed and ready as ever. What a find he was. Mark my words Gaius, Ajax has a glorious future ahead of him and it begins in the arena tomorrow. He will become one of the greats, I am sure of it. Well let us see the action then – on with the fight!" Lucius clapped his hands together and with a whirl of his toga positioned himself a safe distance away from the boys.

"Very well sir. Ajax, Arthur, the fight begins and ends at my command. Is that understood?" Arthur nodded. Ajax, still staring at Arthur through his helmet, crouched slightly and raised his sword arm, ready to strike.

Arthur tested the weight of the net in his hand. He had spent hours with Gaius learning how to cast the net at an opponent to ensnare them, but now that he faced a fully armed gladiator for the first time it felt like a feeble weapon. The trident in his other hand was more reassuring, its length meaning that he should be able to keep Ajax at a safe distance.

Slowly, Ajax began to advance and Arthur felt the familiar rush of blood and adrenalin that always came over him when he was fighting – which was far too often these days. His opponent was far better protected than he was thanks to the shield and helmet, but they looked heavy. Arthur, could move about freely and lightly. In a proper bout, Gaius had said, a retiarius might try to win by making the secutor chase after him for

a long time, draining the heavily laden secutor's energy. But the training arena was not big enough for that.

Ajax was a couple of metres away now, just out of reach of Arthur's trident. Arthur sprang into action, taking a step forward and jabbing with the trident, which clattered into Ajax's shield and glanced off. Arthur's momentum took him a step closer and he had to twist awkwardly away as Ajax thrust at him with his sword.

Heart pounding, Arthur retreated a few steps and once more Ajax began to advance. Arthur threw the net at Ajax's head, then watched in horror as it slid off the smooth helmet and landed on the ground behind his enemy. One weapon lost, Arthur switched the trident to his right hand just as Ajax lunged forwards, holding his shield out before him like a battering ram and crashing into Arthur, who fell heavily to the floor, trapping the trident beneath his own weight.

Ajax towered over him, shield discarded and sword raised in a two handed grip ready to plunge it down. Arthur snatched at his one remaining weapon - the dagger in his belt.

"Enough!" Gaius called, but Ajax paid no heed.

He's going to do it! thought Arthur, panic coursing through his body, and sure enough the sword began to fall. Arthur slashed out with the dagger in the direction of Ajax's feet and felt the blade jar against something hard as his opponent howled in pain, dropping his sword and falling to the floor.

"*I said enough*!" Gaius roared.

Arthur sprang to his feet and retreated away from Ajax as the lanista rushed over to inspect the fallen gladiator.

"Is he injured?" Lucius whined. "Can he still fight tomorrow?"

"I fear not, sir." Gaius shook his head grimly as Ajax writhed around on the floor.

"But we have promised a fight between two young gladiators!" Lucius shouted, his temper flaring. "Am I to look a fool before all of Rome? You boy!" he spat, turning to Arthur. "You are responsible for this outrage so you will fight in his place."

"He is not ready sir," Gaius cautioned.

"Do not question me Gaius! I have made my decision. The boy stabs my finest young gladiator in the foot. He thinks he can fight so tomorrow he fights before all of Rome. The idiot has cost me dearly and he must clear the debt with a great fight tomorrow or else pay the debt with his life."

Arthur felt the blood draining from his head as the words sunk in and the adrenalin dispersed. This was getting wildly out of control. The training arena had been terrifying enough, but fighting at the centre of the amphitheatre in the real arena - and in front of the Roman public? Arthur shivered.

"Steady, boy." Marcus had strolled over to stand beside Arthur and now he called over to Gaius. "Shall I take the boy away while you tend to Ajax, master?" Gaius grunted his assent as a furious Lucius turned and swept across the arena towards the main gates.

"Come with me," said Marcus quietly, and he steered Arthur away from his injured foe and back to his cell.

"You're a smart fighter," said Marcus as Arthur collapsed, shaking, onto his mattress. "For a boy, that is. But they are not right to put you into the arena. You were right to strike at Ajax's feet – he would have killed you – anyone could see that. Lucius is a viper. He has no sense of honour."

"I know how to fight," said Arthur, looking up from his bed and trying to pull himself together enough to seize this opportunity with Marcus. "Not just fighting for sport like this either. Fighting for something real. Fighting for freedom."

"Careful, boy. You can say that to me but if anyone else hears it you could pay with your life. Ever since Spartacus those in charge have been very nervous about gladiators and the idea of freedom."

Arthur knew this might be his only opportunity and carried on, "I've met a lot of warriors you know. That's how I know how to fight. But the best I ever met was a man who fought alongside Spartacus. He died in the end, but what a hero. What a way to die. Fighting to be free instead of doing your master's bidding like a dog. Haven't you ever wanted to do that?"

Marcus gave Arthur a long stare, and nodded. "You remind me of my brother," he said sadly. "There is truth in what you say, but for now you have something else to worry about – surviving in the arena..."

EXTRACT FROM *WARRIOR HEROES*
BY FINN BLADE

GLADIATOR TYPES

To make the fights more interesting gladiators were trained up to be a certain type of fighter who would wear specific types of armour and use specific weapons. This meant that the organisers could pair types of gladiator together knowing that they were evenly matched. There were loads of gladiator types, but here are three different types:

EQUITE

An equite was a gladiator who rode a horse in the arena, based on a mounted Roman cavalryman. He wore a round helmet with a metal grill across his face, a spear that could

be used as a lance or to throw,
a short sword and a small round
shield. Equites only ever fought
other equites in the arena.

RETIARIUS

The easiest gladiator to
recognise, the retiarius wore very
little armour and no helmet or
shield. On the plus side this meant
he could run faster. He carried
a long trident in one hand and a
net in the other, with a dagger in
his belt. The trident was used for
jabbing, and occasionally throwing,
while the net was used either to
tangle his opponent or snatch his
weapon away.

SECUTOR

A secutor only ever fought in
the arena with a retiarius. He had

a smooth helmet with two eye-holes
that was unlikely to get snagged in
a net but which restricted his view
terribly. Otherwise he carried a
large, curved shield and a sword.

CHAPTER 6

Finn stopped, mouth open in awe as a noisy crowd pushed past him in the hot afternoon sun. The vast amphitheatre towered above him, a huge monument to Rome's power, and to fighting. The Professor had told Finn that the Flavian Amphitheatre, or Colosseum, was built for gladiatorial combat but standing before it now Finn could hardly believe his eyes - it looked more like a huge, round palace than a building dedicated to sport. The idea that this vast, beautiful building at the centre of the city was purpose-built for the citizens of Rome to watch people kill one another was both sickening and strangely exciting.

Wresting his eyes down to street level again, Finn could see Titus and his associates making their way through one of the entrances. Quickly Finn darted after them. They had agreed that he would enter the amphitheatre alone so that as few people as possible saw them together. He dashed over to the entrance, waving the ticket that Titus had given him at a harassed looking attendant, then jostled through a narrow passage, hopping up and down to keep Titus in view over the heads of the crowd in front of him.

Remembering Titus' directions, he climbed the steps of the amphitheatre to the third tier. Titus had no gladiators fighting in the games that day and so would be allocated seats high up, further away from the action than Lucius. He climbed the steps until he found the row that his ticket indicated and then walked along it, eyes down, hood up, until he reached his numbered seat. He resolved not to look at Titus, nor look for Lucius, nor even look at the people sitting either side of him for the first few minutes, hoping that any curiosity people felt would disappear as soon as the spectacle began.

Finn had been expecting a bloodthirsty atmosphere but everything seemed very cheerful. Musicians at the edge of the arena were playing a catchy, up-beat tune that carried loudly around the amphitheatre and the whole mood was festive. People around Finn chatted and joked, sharing out snacks and talking about the executions they had witnessed earlier as well as the scheduled fights for that afternoon. He heard Marcus mentioned more than once, though still had no idea when he would be fighting.

As he waited, Finn went over the plan that he and Titus had agreed the previous night. Finn had to find a way of appearing to pour the poison into something Titus would then consume. Titus would then give Finn five minutes to exit the amphitheatre before collapsing and being carried off by his companions, shouting that he had been poisoned. Finn would head back to Lucius' villa and wait for him there to make sure that the show had been noticed.

Dangerous though the scheme was, Finn was reasonably confident that this part of it would go smoothly. It was the next phase that really worried him. The poison Lucius had provided was supposed to kill very quickly and Titus would need to appear dead by the time he got home. But Titus was not willing to continue the pretence for long and had told Finn that he had twenty-four hours to dispose of Lucius one way or another. It was at this point in the plan that Finn's nerves hit a wall. Was he really willing to kill Lucius? Could he poison someone, even a man who deserved it? As he had done many times since the plan had been hatched, Finn turned away from the problem. He would just have to see what opportunities arose once he was back at Lucius' villa.

A roar from the crowd interrupted his anxious thoughts and he looked down at the arena to see the last thing he had expected. A man dressed in a chicken costume was parading around the arena, waving at the crowd! Wrapped up in an assassination plot at the centre of ancient Rome, waiting for the gladiator games to begin, Finn was caught completely off guard by this oddly familiar sight. *I could be at a football match,* he thought to himself, chuckling as someone in a wolf costume bounded into the arena and started chasing the chicken, accompanied by music and roars of laughter from the crowd. The pantomime continued for a few minutes before the wolf caught the chicken and dragged it back down one of the tunnels that led away from the arena.

The music stopped and after a drum roll an official began to call out an announcement, but as Finn's eyes sought the caller out they came to rest on something that brought the reality of his situation back into focus. Staring straight back at him from several rows down was the man he knew he would have to kill. Lucius held his gaze for a few moments, then turned and sat down. There had been something knowing in Lucius' stare and Finn bit his lip anxiously. Lucius couldn't know that Finn and Titus were planning to turn the tables on him, could he?

Suddenly Finn jumped as a loud bang was followed by the clattering of hooves, and two gladiators on horseback cantered into the arena. Both were armed with long spears and small shields, with swords in their belts.

"Our entertainment today begins with a duel between two equites and for your entertainment their owner Lucius has stated that they may fight to the death," the caller announced to gasps from the crowd. "On the white horse, making his first appearance in the Flavian Amphitheatre, Achilles!" The crowd cheered and clapped as Achilles, dressed in a white tunic to match his white horse, cantered around the edge of the arena with his spear held aloft.

"And on the black horse, needing no introduction to the people of this city, victorious in every bout he has fought, famed across the empire and here today to fight gloriously once again for the citizens of Rome..." the caller drew breath and threw back his head, *"Marcus!"* The crowd screamed their approval as Finn got his first look at the man he was here to help, albeit behind a helmet. Marcus trotted slowly around the arena, his calm bearing as menacing as his black horse and tunic.

Finn had expected to find the games disturbing, but as the thousands of people in the amphitheatre rose to their feet and began chanting Marcus' name Finn found himself on his feet as well, completely caught up with everyone else in anticipation of the fight to come. *Arthur would love this,* thought Finn, wondering what it must be like to have a stadium full of people chanting your name before you begin mortal combat with another warrior. If a gladiator was a champion like this Finn could see why he might not want to escape. Yet Marcus did not appear to revel in the attention. He seemed calm, still and centred, in stark contrast to Achilles who was twisting around in his saddle, tensing and re-tensing his muscles as if fighting something already.

"Gladiators, to the tunnels!" came the call. The two men rode off in opposite directions and disappeared out of the arena into two different tunnels, heavy doors closing behind them. A slow, heavy drumbeat began and the crowd fell quiet. The drums grew louder and louder, the sound booming fiercely around the arena until Finn could feel it pounding in his chest. His pulse quickened. The crowd stared down expectantly. The doors snapped open again, the crowd bellowed and the riders galloped out of the tunnels towards one another, covering the distance to the middle of the arena in a flash

with arms bent and spears held at shoulder height. Both thrust forward as they came together and both parried with their shields, clattering off one another and slowing as they reached the opposite sides of the arena again. They circled clockwise and the noise from the crowd dipped a little, then rose again as Achilles made the first move and began his charge. Marcus responded immediately and again the riders tore across the arena to crash spears against shields and again neither rider fell.

Again and again they charged, each time to a roaring crescendo from the crowd until at last Marcus caught Achilles with a glancing blow to the shield arm, drawing blood from his opponent and frenzied shouts of encouragement from the crowd. Achilles was knocked back in his saddle but stayed on his horse and wheeled around immediately to face Marcus again.

This time Marcus charged and Achilles waited for him. Sensing a climax the crowd cheered Marcus forward, but Achilles had a surprise in store. When Marcus was still ten metres away Achilles threw his spear. The black horse reared up as the spear sailed past its nose. Twisting out of the spear's path, Marcus fell heavily onto the sand of the arena. Achilles leapt off his horse as Marcus staggered to his feet, casting his spear to one side. Both men drew their swords and rushed to clash again, this time on foot.

The blades flashed in the fierce sunlight and as they met each blow rang out around the arena, drawing gasps and cheers and groans from the audience. Achilles, who was apparently unknown to the crowd, was swiftly earning their respect as he matched Marcus blow for blow. It was a frenzied duel, neither man giving or taking any chance to slow the tempo and Finn felt sure that it must end soon. It suddenly occurred to him that if Marcus were killed he and Arthur would have failed in their mission to help his ghost – something that had never happened before in all their adventures. *What would happen then? Would they be stuck in Rome forever?*

But he need not have worried. The wound in Achilles' arm was beginning to take its toll on the gladiator and Marcus began to beat him back towards the edge of the arena. Moments later Achilles was down on one knee, fending off overhead blows until his sword was smashed from his grip by a particularly savage strike.

He lifted one arm in the air with forefinger extended to signify his surrender and the crowd went wild.

It dawned on Finn that this would be a good moment to make his move, while the crowd were so pumped up. He scurried along the row of seats to his left in the direction that he knew Titus was sitting.

"*The victory belongs to Marcus,*" cried the announcer, as Finn caught sight of his conspirator.

"*And what of Achilles?*" the announcer went on. The crowd cheered and called Achilles' name, clearly impressed by the strength he had shown.

"*Will he live or will he die?*" Down on the floor of the arena Finn saw Marcus standing over Achilles, sword still raised.

"*Live! Live! Live!*" chanted the crowd as Finn brushed past the last few people separating him from Titus.

"*The people have spoken. Achilles lives!*" A great cheer went up and at that moment Finn bumped heavily into Titus and reached a hand out as if to steady himself, grabbing Titus' wrist just above a cup that he was holding.

"Get away!" Titus shouted, pushing him roughly back in the direction he had come from. Finn did as he was told, retreating back towards his seat. He glanced down at Lucius and met his stare once more. Titus was shouting obscenities after him and, though he could not be sure, Finn thought he saw a smile flicker across Lucius' face.

EXTRACT FROM *WARRIOR HEROES*
BY FINN BLADE

A DAY AT THE GAMES

Games at the arena were advertised
on billboards around the city, and
programmes were sold announcing the
schedule for the day, which usually
went something like this:

- Bestiari - gladiators vs wild
  animals

- Executions of criminals or duels
  between prisoners of war

- Bouts between gladiators

The games were a way for the
wealthy and powerful to show their
generosity towards the public and
keep them on their side, so they
were almost always free to attend.
The day would often begin with some

pantomime and music, and the crowd
would often be given treats to eat.

THE BIG STAGE

The arenas were sandpits about the
size of football pitches, surrounded
by rising circular rows of seats,
just like sports stadiums today.
The most famous was the Flavian
Amphitheatre, or Colosseum as we
know it today. This huge building in
the centre of Rome could hold over
50,000 people and was purpose built
for gladiator games.

CHAPTER 7

The nervous excitement Finn felt at having pulled off the first part of the plan wore off the further he got from the amphitheatre, and as he approached Lucius' villa, the question he had been avoiding rose again in his mind. Could he really poison someone? It was one thing defending yourself against an attacker in the heat of battle, but quite another to plan a cold-blooded, secretive assassination. That felt more like, well, murder.

On the other hand Lucius had more or less threatened to kill both him and Arthur, and it was hard to see Marcus suddenly deciding that he wanted to escape unless something dramatic happened. Also Finn was worried about Arthur. He knew that deep down his brother was loving pretending to be a gladiator, but the more time he spent in Gaius' school, the more likely it was he would be seriously hurt, regardless of Lucius.

As Finn arrived at the villa he still did not know what he was going to do beyond telling Lucius that Titus was poisoned. He walked over to the small side door he and Gaius had used the previous evening and one of the guards accompanied him into the courtyard, calling out so that the silent slave appeared. The slave motioned for Finn to follow him into the house and then into the same room in which he had first met Lucius. Finn sat down on a bench and waited, staring with loathing at a bust of Lucius that decorated a small alcove.

It wasn't long before another disturbing idea presented itself. If Lucius did believe that Titus was now poisoned then what use was Finn to him? In fact, wasn't it in Lucius' interests to get rid of Finn altogether - destroying the evidence? Just at that moment the door to the room swung open and Finn held his breath, before sighing with relief when Lucilla walked in.

"What happened?" She asked in barely more than a whisper as she made her way quickly over to where he was sitting.

Finn, grateful to have one person he could confide in, told her the whole story of his instructions to poison Titus and of the plot to fool Lucius into believing this had happened. The girl listened carefully, and when he had finished she thought for a while.

"So Titus was willing to help as long as you... dispose of Lucius quickly?"

"That's how he put it, yes, but what am I going to do?" said Finn miserably. "The only plan that makes sense is to kill him and I don't know if I can do it." As soon as the words were out of his mouth Finn regretted them. How could he have been so stupid as to say that in this place, and to Lucilla?

"Give me the poison," said Lucilla, her face drawn. "I will do it." Finn couldn't believe what he was hearing. "I hate him and I want revenge," she hissed. "And if he lives then I will have to stay here with him – from what you've told me I now know that the marriage to Titus was obviously never going to happen."

"It's too dangerous," said Finn, his brow creased.

"Finn, you have played your part. Now give me the poison and get back to your brother. What do you think my uncle's plans will be for you now that he thinks you've done his dirty work? He's ruthless Finn, he kills anyone who is a threat..."

Finn knew she was right but it felt very strange as he pulled the bottle from around his neck and handed it over...

* * *

When Gaius brought Marcus back to the school at the end of the day Arthur was relieved to learn that the gladiator had won his bout. Arthur had been practising with his net and trident on and off for most of the day. He fervently hoped that somehow Lucius would change his mind about sending Arthur into the arena for the bout that Ajax had been scheduled to fight the following day at the games, but he had seen and heard enough of the cruel senator by then to know that this was unlikely. By his own reckoning there were only two ways he was going to escape fighting, and probably dying, in the arena. If Titus and Finn's plot had worked then there was a slim chance that Lucius would be dead by now. Otherwise the only realistic chance he had was to appeal to Marcus' sense of honour, and to his belief that it was unfair to make an untrained boy fight in the arena, and persuade him to escape Rome tonight.

All the trainees and gladiators in the school were summoned to the training arena to hear

Gaius announce the day's winners and losers. There were cheers for the victors but little emotion spared for those who had died. Arthur got the sense that nobody wanted to think about the reality of gladiators dying in the arena, even though it was something that must have haunted all of them constantly. After the formality of these announcements, the men were told to wash and prepare themselves for a feast that Lucius would be providing. Arthur dashed across to Marcus before he could disappear, thinking quickly.

"Congratulations!" he said. "You won!"

"I always do," was the simple reply. "I thought of you today Arthur and there is something I want to show you. Go and wait in your cell and I will be there soon."

Arthur fizzed with energy. This was his first real chance to talk with Marcus of escape. His excitement mounted still further when he found Finn back at the cell. In hoarse whispers they filled each other in on the day's events. Arthur's eyes widened at the news that Lucilla was planning to kill her uncle, and Finn's jaw tightened when he heard that Lucius intended to make Arthur fight in the amphitheatre. Finn quickly agreed that they must somehow persuade Marcus to escape with them that night, and when the gladiator stooped to enter the cell they were primed and ready.

Arthur introduced his brother, and Finn explained that he had been in the amphitheatre and had seen Marcus fight.

"I heard that you two were brothers," said Marcus. "But I thought it strange that we never saw you training. Why has Gaius brought you here if not to fight? They are usually happy enough to separate families."

The brothers looked at one another nervously, not sure how much to divulge, until Finn shrugged.

"I have chosen to be honest with two people already and they have helped me," he began, and keeping his voice low Finn told his story again. Marcus listened intently, his brow furrowing when Finn told him that Lucius had adopted Lucilla after murdering her parents, and further still at the news that Lucius wanted to use Finn as an assassin.

For a long time after Finn had finished Marcus

said nothing, and the boys began to worry that they had misjudged the situation and made a mistake in being so open.

"Let us hope that the girl succeeds in ridding us of this sick animal," said Marcus eventually. "The world will be a better place without him. What sort of man sends boys to kill his rivals? What sort of man kills a child's parents and then tries to become their father? And what sort of man sends an untrained youth into the arena to fight with gladiators? He has no honour, and nor do thousands of others like him in Rome. My brother was right..." he paused and put a hand to his chest. Something hung there from a cord around his neck and he pulled it over his head. In his open palm the boys saw a tiny wooden carving of a warrior on horseback.

"I too had a brother once," he went on slowly. "He was some years younger than me when we were sold into slavery. I was fully grown and a lanista spotted me and bought me to train as a gladiator. By luck I was able to persuade him that my brother was also destined to be a fighter and he took a chance and bought my brother too, although he was not much older than you Arthur. The first day that I fought in the arena my brother gave me this carving for luck, and I have never lost. There is something very special between brothers who really believe in each other." He paused and looked up at the ceiling.

"I was always the better fighter, but he had the bigger heart. When news reached us of Spartacus my brother saw something that I did not. He saw a chance to live as a free man. But I saw only certain death. We argued and argued and eventually I made him swear that he would not join Spartacus. He swore, but I could see in his eyes that it went against everything in his spirit. I woke one morning to find him gone. Years later I learned that he had become one of Spartacus' most trusted soldiers. I knew then that he must be dead and ever since that day I have cursed myself for not knowing him better. I should never have made him swear to stay. It should have been the other way around – I should have been encouraging him to reclaim his freedom. Perhaps I should have even gone with him... And now I learn that the man who *claims* to own me is even more of a monster than I thought."

"Marcus," said Finn gently. "Your life isn't over you know. You can't bring your brother back but you can stand up to Lucius. You can help us stop him. And you can follow your brother in spirit by escaping with us and living as a free man somewhere. We have to escape – Arthur is not ready to fight in the arena and I... I am as good as dead if Lucius lives."

Marcus stared at Finn, his eyes burning.

"Come with us and honour your brother," Finn went on. "Come with us and help two brothers escape and survive together."

There was fire in Marcus' eyes as he opened his mouth to reply, but the words died on his lips as the door to the boys' room opened and Gaius entered, followed by a thinly smiling Lucius and an ashen-faced Lucilla.

CHAPTER 8

Marcus and the boys jumped to their feet immediately.

"Excellent, excellent," Lucius drawled. "I thought I should congratulate Marcus personally before the feast. I confess I am surprised to find you here Marcus. These boys are far beneath the standing of a champion like you, surely! But no matter," he went on, clearly not expecting a reply.

"I have something to discuss with the boys also." His eyes narrowed as he said this, and Lucilla's face behind him screamed a silent warning at Finn.

"Finn, you were there to witness Marcus win yet another bout in the arena. He was magnificent, was he not? Of course you will also have the pleasure of watching your brother in combat tomorrow before the citizens of Rome. Although one does not sense that his chances of victory are high."

"But I did as you..."

"Silence!" Lucius hissed, and behind him Lucilla shook her head frantically. "Your brother has a debt to pay. He injured Ajax, one of my finest, and the young brute may never fight again for all we know. The boy has to pay."

"Sir, the people will not look favourably on an unfair match," Gaius remarked.

"The match will be fair enough," Lucius replied, sneering at Finn. "What could be fairer than a fight between two brothers?"

An eerie silence filled the cell as everyone stared at Lucius.

"But I did what you told me to do!" Finn blurted out.

"You did no such thing!" Lucius screamed, lashing out and slapping Finn hard across the mouth. "Titus is no closer to death than he was yesterday, whatever your little ruse may have suggested. And do not try to deny it, I have sources close to Titus. Did you - a wretch we picked out of the gutter - did you really think that I would not find out?

I have seen off more enemies, and lived through more attempts on my life than you can comprehend!

"You did not poison Titus, he feigned his own death to deceive me which means that he is plotting something, and you are part of the plot no doubt. Well, we will see what to do with you if you survive in the arena tomorrow but it will be a fight to the death... I promise you that." Lucius paused to appreciate the looks of horror on the boys' faces.

"Now," he went on. "In case you have plans for that poison, where is the bottle?"

"I don't have it," Finn replied with a shrug.

"It was not used today so where is it?" Lucius roared, leaping forward and grabbing Finn by the throat. Marcus stepped towards

them but was ordered back with a barked command from Gaius, who had drawn his sword. Finn shook his head as his ears started to ring.

"Tell me or I will kill you now!"

"Stop!" Lucilla cried. "Stop it. I have the poison and it was I who intended to use it to give you the death that you have given so many others. Only I would have had the courage to do it myself and not found someone else to do it for me like you have done countless times before!"

Lucius dropped Finn like a stone and spun around, his face white with fury.

"I should have killed you when I killed your parents," he spat as his hand closed around the girl's throat.

"No matter," Lucius snarled, his hand still wrapped around Lucilla's throat. "There is still time for me to correct my mistake."

"Sir, not the girl..." began Gaius.

"Hold your tongue, fool! It was you who brought the boy to me. For all I know you are part of the plot." Lucilla gripped her uncle's hand, a look of panic spreading across her face. Marcus could hold back no longer. He leapt at Gaius and with one vicious punch laid him out cold on the floor.

"Let her go or you die Lucius," he growled, picking up the lanista's sword.

"Kill me?" Lucius howled with laughter. "A gladiator and a slave would dare to kill a senator of Rome? This little scorpion planned to kill me, you heard – "

His words turned to a high-pitched groan as Marcus lunged and thrust forward savagely, burying his sword in Lucius' back. The girl fell gasping to the floor while Marcus stood behind the senator and pushed him away, causing him to topple forward off the sword. He lay wheezing and whimpering, clutching at his wound for a moment until he became completely still. Lucilla hauled herself to her feet, looked down at him and spat before staggering backwards and falling against a wall.

Lucilla and the boys were too stunned to speak, but Marcus acted instantly, instructing them to wait in the cell while he fetched what they would need, and striding away before they could argue. Arthur was the next to regain his composure, casting around for something to tie Gaius' hands with.

"We won't have much chance if he wakes up while Marcus is away," he explained, removing the lanista's belt and binding it tightly around the big man's wrists.

"Wh... What..." Lucilla stammered, staring down at Lucius' now motionless body. "He's dead. What will we do?"

"We run. We get out of Rome with Marcus before the body is discovered. Gaius heard everything and he was loyal to Lucius, although I don't think he liked him much."

"Nobody liked him," said Lucilla bitterly. "But if a senator is killed someone has to pay... How do we know Marcus has not already accused us?"

But at that moment Marcus reappeared with a bundle of cloaks and swords. He stepped briskly into the cell.

"Freedom, you say?"

EXTRACT FROM *WARRIOR HEROES*
BY FINN BLADE

ORIGINS OF THE GLADIATORS

SACRIFICE

The idea of making two people
fight to the death in front of a
crowd wasn't actually a Roman idea.
The Greeks did it, and so did the
Etruscans who lived near Rome in the
early days. They used to get people
fighting to the death as a sacrifice
at a funeral, and the Romans picked
up the idea and ran with it.

FUNERALS

It became fashionable for wealthy
Roman families to organise these
funeral duels, and soon people
started getting carried away. The
spectacle grew and grew until at

the biggest funerals of very wealthy people you might get more than fifty duels.

PUBLIC SPECTACLES

These funeral games were usually played out in public places like fields and market squares where you might see a carnival today. As Roman people got a serious appetite for watching people kill each other they began to build huge stadiums, a lot like football stadiums today, so that thousands of people could watch the games.

BLOODLUST

Eventually it became such big business, and a good gladiator could make so much money for his owner, that they weren't expected to kill each other anymore, just to fight really well. Of course people still wanted to see some blood, so the Romans would execute prisoners, or get prisoners of war to fight to the death before the proper Gladiator bouts began later in the day.

CHAPTER 9

As they stood at the gladiator school gates looking out into the fading evening light the group of four pulled their hoods up over their heads and checked that their swords were secure under their cloaks. Marcus had told some of the other gladiators that he and the boys had been instructed to take Lucilla back to her father's villa, and that Gaius and Lucius had some business to discuss before the feast began.

"We have little time," Marcus muttered. "They will be after us soon enough and we must hurry. We will make for the Tiber and bribe a boatman to take us along the river out of the city overnight. With luck we will be out of Rome before the search is on." But even as Marcus said this, a shout went up inside the school.

"Follow me," he barked. *"Run!"* They dashed after Marcus, heading towards the centre of the city.

"They're coming," Finn cried hoarsely as Gaius and a small group of gladiators spilled out into the street behind them. The fugitives dodged past pedestrians and carts and sprinted onto a bigger road, drawing stares and curses from the people they passed so that the people ahead of them began to turn and stare also. Some way along the road, two mounted soldiers turned to see what the commotion was about.

"Urban guards!" Lucilla gasped. "Marcus, I know somewhere we can hide." Marcus nodded and the girl took the lead, darting off the main road and into one of the labyrinths of alleyways that had been the boys' first experience of Rome. The group shoved past beggars and night-hawkers, twisting and turning through the stinking alleys until Finn and Arthur were completely lost and could only follow blindly, praying that Lucilla was right. She stopped outside a completely anonymous door and banged at it, leaning her head against the wood and gasping for air.

"We don't have long," Marcus warned as the seconds ticked past. They could not hear any pursuers but their flight had hardly been inconspicuous.

"I wondered when I'd next run into you boys," somebody said from behind them in the dark alley, and Arthur's shoulders sank.

"Festus," he replied wearily as he and the others turned around. "It had to be you..."

"We've got a score to settle, boy!" said Festus, and the gang behind him muttered their approval.

"Well you can settle it with me," Marcus growled, barging to the front. The change in Festus' expression was almost comical.

"You're... You're a gladiator aren't you?" Festus couldn't disguise the awe in his voice. "You're Marcus the equite! I saw you in the arena today!"

"Then you know better than to pick a fight with my friends."

"These are your friends?" Festus sounded confused and Marcus seized the initiative.

"I have a proposition for you. How would you and your gang of kids here like to say one day that you helped a gladiator fight his way out of Rome?"

* * *

An hour had passed by the time they were ready. Festus, it came as no surprise, was a huge fan of all gladiators and had watched Marcus fighting in the arena on numerous occasions. Festus and the gang were all too happy to forego their grudge against Arthur if it meant they could help one of their heroes, and he had led the fugitives to a small, empty house where they had hidden in a dark room while he went to make the arrangements that would get them to a boat on the Tiber, taking with him a bag of coins that Marcus handed over.

Finn had expressed serious doubts about trusting Festus, but Marcus and Lucilla agreed that there was no choice. The urban guards would be looking for them all over the city by now and unless they were to split up, which none of them wanted, they would need all the help they could find to get out of Rome alive.

"Giving him money was a mistake," said Finn.

"I had to give him money to buy us a boatman willing to take the risk," Marcus replied. "In any case, I've won enough bouts in the arena that I am not short of money. I can afford to lose some."

A grinding noise outside the house set everyone's nerves on edge, but Arthur, peering through a crack in the door, soon reassured them that it was Festus, accompanied by one of his gang who was hauling a cart along the alley.

"We have a plan that should work," Festus announced proudly. "It's dark now and there is a boat waiting for you. The guards are searching for four people but Marcus and the girl are the recognisable ones so they will need to be hidden. We will be using the cart to hide them, and the boys can pull it."

"The urban guards are not stupid," Marcus retorted. "They will be searching anyone and everyone, and two boys pulling a vegetable cart will be enough to warrant a search."

"True," said Festus with a grin. "But this is no vegetable cart." He led them outside and lifted a large piece of sack cloth. Lucilla stifled a scream with her hand. Staring back at them from the cart were five dead bodies.

"The best way for you to get out alive..." said Festus. "Pretend to be dead."

"I can't... I can't lie on them..." Lucilla whispered.

"You won't lie on them," replied Festus with a wicked grin. "You'll need to lie under them."

Despite Lucilla's protestations Marcus and the boys knew that Festus was right. A cartload of dead bodies destined for a public grave was less likely to provoke unwelcome interest from the guards than anything else. They lifted the bodies aside to make space for Marcus and then cajoled Lucilla to lie next to him, her face buried in her hands, before placing a second layer of sacking on top of their friends, followed by the bodies.

"One more thing," said Festus. "My boys are positioned along the route to the river and as we pass them they will follow. When we get to the boat we'll be there to distract any guards who might take an interest."

"You've done well boy," came Marcus' muffled voice. "I'm sure you kept some of the money I gave you for the boatman?"

"Of course!" Festus grinned, and they heard Marcus chuckle.

"Festus," Arthur added. "Thanks. I thought you would turn us in."

"If it was just you I would have, but him?" Festus nodded at the cart and began to stroll away. "He was already a hero on these streets.

Now he's killed one of the most hated men in Rome and most people will thank him for it. Follow after me, but keep your distance so I can warn you of any trouble."

Arthur and Finn got into position at the front of the cart, lifted the yoke and began to pull. The cart was heavy and it took a big heave to get it going, but once the wheels were rolling the boys were able to keep pace with Festus easily enough. Festus kept to the alleys for as long as possible, but eventually he led them onto a larger and much busier road.

"What do we say if we're stopped?" said Arthur suddenly. "We don't know where we're supposed to be heading!"

"Stop a moment!" someone hissed behind them and the boys froze, the cart knocking into them from behind. It was a few moments before Finn realised the voice had come from inside the cart.

"Esquiline Hill. That's where the mass funerals happen." There was something very creepy about hearing those words come from a cartload of corpses, and Finn shivered, grateful all of a sudden that he was pulling the cart, and not in it. Looking back, Finn recognised some of Festus' gang strolling along behind them. The boys resumed their progress with another heave, and soon noticed that they were heading slightly downhill. Ahead of Festus the boys could now see the black scar of the river for the first time, and the incline steepened. Suddenly they found that they needed to pull back on the yoke rather than push against it as gravity began to drag the cart downhill. Finn's foot slipped in the mud and he stumbled backwards, throwing Arthur off balance in turn. The cart quickened and the boys scrambled back into position, knowing that if it ran away from them then Lucilla and Marcus would almost certainly be discovered. As they struggled to regain control, Arthur glanced ahead and swore.

"Guards! Festus is talking to a bunch of guards. What's he doing?"

"Calm down," his brother urged. "If he wanted to turn us in he would have done it already. He's trying to distract them. Just keep walking past them." As they drew nearer one of the guards turned and stared at them

before breaking away from the others just as the cart drew level. Finn and Arthur stared intently at the road in front of them and carried on, until Finn could not help glancing round.

The soldier was walking along beside the cart with one hand on the sack cloth. He lifted it up and Finn held his breath, waiting for the inevitable shout.

But the soldier merely wrinkled his nose and dropped the cloth, turning back to the other guards. Moments later Festus reappeared in front and led them on, the boys glancing wide-eyed at one another, too tense to notice the stench of sewage that drifted towards them as they approached the river. Just as the road they were on was about to lead them onto a bridge, Festus turned and headed along a lane that followed the river bank and brought them to a flight of steps, at the bottom of which a small barge was moored.

Finn and Arthur set the cart down, bursting with excitement now the promise of escape was so near while Festus, saying nothing, made his way to the back of the cart.

"Oh no!" Finn breathed, the blood draining

from his face. Turning off the main road and beginning to run towards them were two of the guards that Festus had been talking to.

"You there!" One of them called. "Stay where you are!"

CHAPTER 10

Finn and Arthur froze as Festus put his fingers to his lips, whistled loudly, then turned and bolted along the riverside. The guards ran towards them, swords drawn and raised while down in the barge a black-cloaked boatman emerged and began untying his moorings frantically.

"Marcus," Arthur hissed. "Guards! Jump out on my call."

Up on the bridge a great commotion broke out and for a moment the boys thought that more people were coming for them. Then some of the wooden stalls on the bridge went up in flames and in the sudden light Festus' gang could be seen dancing around, pushing and shoving everyone within reach.

"He's creating a decoy!" said Finn, breathlessly as the guards approached.

"You boys," one of them barked. "Take two steps away from the cart. Run and you will die." They did as they were told and the guards rushed to the back of the cart and tore off the cover. In seconds they had dragged the five bodies onto the ground and exposed the final covering.

"Now!" yelled Arthur, pulling back his own cloak and reaching for the short sword that Marcus had given him earlier. Finn did the same just as Marcus leapt up to a crouch in the cart.

"You are outnumbered," Finn began, but Marcus was in no mood to negotiate. He leapt down with a cry, punching the hilt of the sword into one man and knocking him into the other so that both collapsed to the ground. Two quick thrusts followed, and moments later Marcus was dragging the bodies down the steps and flinging them in the river before the terrified stare of the boatman.

"Time to earn your money, old man," said Marcus and he beckoned the boys down. Finn helped Lucilla out of the cart and all four of them made their way down to the barge, running swiftly to the bow and lying down on their backs so that they could not be seen from land. The boatman said nothing, just pushed away from the bank with a long pole and steered them out towards the middle of the river where the current began to take them slowly away from the bridge.

None of them could have said how long they lay like that, silently waiting for the call that would announce the boat was to be searched by more guards, but the sounds of the city gradually diminished until all they could hear was the blowing of the wind, the lapping of the water, and the steady wooden thud of the boatman's pole against the side of the boat.

The moon shone through wispy clouds, casting just enough faint light to illuminate Marcus' face staring up at the sky. When Finn turned to look at the gladiator something burned in the man's eyes.

"You're a free man," said Finn.

"Yes," said Marcus, glancing over at Lucilla who had fallen into a fitful sleep. "And now at last I have something to protect again."

The moon disappeared again as the boat entered a thick river mist and they were plunged into total darkness. Finn reached out to hold Arthur's arm as he felt the spinning sensation that heralded the end of another adventure, and then the shapes of furniture in the Professor's study began to materialise out of the darkness...

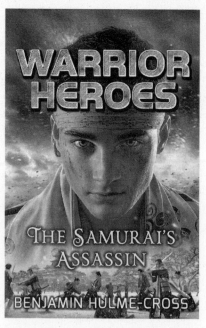

WARRIOR HEROES
The Samurai's Assassin

Benjamin Hulme-Cross

Trapped in their great grandfather's museum
and visited by the restless ghosts of warriors past,
Arthur and Finn must travel back in time and
rewrite history to set the ghosts free. Will the boys
put a stop to the powerful warlord Kenji Kuroda
seizing power once and for all?

£4.99

9781472904669

Extract from
WARRIOR HEROES
The Samurai's Assassin

Finn drifted lazily towards consciousness, dreaming that he was leaping to impossible heights and then rushing back down to earth, only to leap even higher into the air once more. He licked his lips and tasted brine, noting that heavy rain was pelting his back as he took another giant leap skywards. It was just as he reached the highest point of the arc and hung there for a moment, waiting for the fall that he woke with a jolt.

A huge wave rolled forward and Finn swooped down the back of it, slipping off a plank of wood that he had been half-lying on and gulping down a mouthful of sea water as he shouted out in panic. Spluttering, he kicked and hoisted himself back onto the tiny float, at the same time trying to blink and shake the water out of his eyes before the next wave began to lift him up again. As he reached the top of the wave he twisted around, praying he would see some way out of this nightmare that he had swapped for the Professor's study. He felt marginally better when he saw that the waves were surging towards land and that he was in the middle of a small bay.

Finn pulled himself further forward on the plank, as if he were lying on a surfboard, and as he rose with the next wave he pushed himself up on his arms to get a better view. He could see very little of the shoreline through the torrent

About the author

Growing up in London I spent a lot of time sitting on the Underground, daydreaming and reading books. Historical adventures in far-flung lands were always my favourite and I used to love visiting castles and ruins.

After I left home I lived in Japan for a while and learned all about the Samurai. Now I've swapped the city for the countryside, and as well as reading books I also write stories and plays for young people.

The thing I like most about being a writer is playing around with ideas for stories in my head, which is daydreaming really so not much has changed!

of rain, but what he did see turned his stomach and the feeling of relief he had felt just moments ago quickly evaporated. The huge rollers were breaking over a line of jagged rocks that stuck up out of the sea like teeth, and he was heading straight for them.